The Akalango Dream

Written by

Lauretta Ofulue

The Akalango Dream

Written by

Lauretta Ofulue

Publisher's page

Photo credit: www.pixabay.com

Copyright

Otitodilichukwu
Glory be to God

Table of contents

Chapter 1

The Day of Reckoning

"I have come here regarding your brother Delis. He has offended our master and today he is wanted for reckoning. The Akalango master needs his soul because today the day of reckoning has come. It is here for him at last and he knows it."

Elder Dumayi was the one who answered the door when the strange sounding man came requesting to collect Delis. Our elder brother Delis was always notorious. Always getting himself into trouble. He was mixed up in many runs, deals and even shootouts. He was just trouble personified.

This evening was the end of the day to what had been a family get-together. All the members of our family were present. I was in the room with my son who had just finally gone to sleep. My sister's children were somewhere playing. I could hear their noisy chattering. Cousin Sumy with my younger brother Joromi and the rest of the family were in the main living room watching a game of football. The doorbell had rung and the women in the kitchen screamed for someone to get it before the baby- my baby woke up.

It had been a beehive of activities that day. Bros Sparkie as we called one of the elder uncles was going back to the USA that weekend, so every member of the family had come to send him off as was customary for us.

"Papa P wants Delis today," the strange man said.

I could hear him speaking in our corridor past elder Dumayi and there seemed to be a scuffle in the corridor. I tiptoed towards the door to the room where I was and closed it shut. It was so scary. The house seemed to drop into a state of silence. I could literally hear everyone's heartbeat.

"What has Delis done again?" I wondered.

"Who on earth had he offended this time?" My heart was beating so fast.

I heard footsteps...

They got closer...

But thankfully, it was that of all the women and children. The door opened and they filed into the room. Each person looked horror stricken. My uncles were still in the living room. But what was also worrying was that elder Dumayi and the stranger seemed to go silent as well. I could not understand.

"I am giving you five minutes to produce Delis," the stranger said.

"There is no one called Delis here," elder Dumayi replied.

"The hourglass has turned," the stranger said and then fell silent.

At that instant, we all looked at the clock like soldiers on parade with their eyes to the right - It was 6.25 p.m.

Chapter 2

The Arrival

No one made a sound. Not even the men in the living room. I desperately prayed for my baby not to wake up screaming.

About a minute later, Delis waltzed in through the door having no idea what he had walked into.

"Delis! Delis!" I heard elder Dumayi saying.

"Leave this place now!"

Then, footsteps - quick footsteps were all I heard as Delis ran off.

"Hahahahahahahahahahahahahahaha," the strange man laughed.

"Two more minutes left for you to submit him by yourself," he warned sternly.

Silence..........

It felt like the longest silence ever.

"Now old man since you have refused to submit Delis to grand master Akalango, I have knowingly seen that you sighted him and deliberately made him unavailable to the Lord master for his reckon day as beknowest to him. The reckoning therefore doth resteth on you. You "oleman have carried the pot of recompense on thy head!" he blurted out scarily.

In the small room, we all grabbed one another in horror. All my aunties, sisters, cousins, and mom where gasping. I put my finger on my lips gesturing for them to stay quiet. Even I could not make sense of the gibberish the man just spat out of his mouth in the name of speech.

Grand master? Reckoning? Beknowest? What was all this about?

Elder Dumayi, as we all called my dad's eldest brother laughed.

"Hahahahahahahahaha...no chance!" he said.

At that instant, my mum opened the door so she could see what was happening and I joined her as well. Then I saw my uncles Charlis and Peero rush into the corridor. Before the strange messenger man could turn his face, they pounced on him punching and kicking him. I ran back into the room. The man was screaming. I looked at the children whose heads were all dug into the pillows and duvets in fear. The sounds were horrifying.

"Turn up that music," I heard my father say from the living room.

They were still pounding that man. His screams quietened into shrieks.

"Reckoning what?" Uncle Charlis said, as he dealt him yet another blow.

"Taking who?" Uncle Peero added.

"We will finish you today," elder Dumayi said.

"Lord master wants to recompense who?" Uncle Charlis said, and with that they all burst into laughter.

"Why did you not give the stupid Delis to him when he ran in earlier my mother said?" she was still watching from the doorway.

"Shut up woman," elder Dumayi replied.

"This is not a matter for women," he added sharply. At this point I became worried because I could not hear any sound from the man being tortured.

"He is dead oo," elder Dumayi said, a bit triumphantly.

"The foolish guy, he thought he could rattle us! get that large trunk box and we will put him there before he gets stiff." Elder Dumayi said it like he had done this before.

I was in shock. What had we just heard.... Or better still witnessed. A murder?

The kids....

Oh my God!! the kids heard it all!

Chapter 3

The Clear up

It was supposed to be a happy day. I realised that nobody had still moved from the living room. It was as if we all knew our positions and it felt like somehow pretending we were not there kind of made us absent - less guilty... not witnesses.

“Put him in Sparkie’s trunk and I will give you further instructions,” I heard elder Dumayi saying.

I don’t know what even scared me more at this point. The crime or the expert way elder Dumayi was handling it. He was just too composed, and I hated to admit that it felt like an activity he had the mastery of.

"Sparkie’s car is not here in the driveway,” Uncle Charlis said.

Well, that was because Sparkie had taken some of our cousins home earlier. They all seemed to have forgotten.

“Let’s use Kolo’s car,” elder Dumayi suggested.

“No way,” I heard my dad scream from the other end of the corridor towards the living room.

“And rope him in?” my dad asked with a hint of fear in his voice.

"True that," said elder Dumayi.

"Then we have to go traditional," elder Dumayi announced.

"We will do it the old El-dee way," elder Dumayi said.

At this point I was sure that he must have been a killer himself. My uncle... A killer?... I could not even bear the thought.

"Get a trolley and you guys will push him, you have to powder your hands. Get Soki's powder here," elder Dumayi instructed.

"No chance," that was my petrified father again.

"There is nothing like Soki's powder here. There is powder... Can you all stop calling names?" my dad screamed.

"You always were weak Semante," elder Dumayi said to my dad.

"Oh dear, even my name too! Seriously?" My dad raged.

"Elder, trolley is ready o," Uncle Charlis said. I could hear a trolley scrape the ground now.

"Good Charlo! Now Peero let's lift the trunk box into it. I will say the blessings for the journey to seal the deal. I heard elder Dumayi's footsteps some minutes later as he came back with things that sounded like coins and plates. Whatever they were, they clattered as he brought them.

"Now first things first," he said. "We call his name."

"But we no know him name elder D," Peero said.

"Why ya worry man?" elder Dumayi replied.

"Dem ah no call me El-dee for nuttin bwaay," he said.

"I search de eyes of Kolanga for im name and im ma tell me now, aarite? Worri nat man," our Elder Dumayi said.

It was getting worse. Elder Dumayi seemed to be a cultist!

Then he screamed.

"Sokoni....Sokoni...me call ya! You alive in dat trunk you answer, you dead as cold meat, you stay dumb forever man."

"Sokoni...Sokoni...for one last time.... You dey there?

"Me hear you loud and clear sir!"

I nearly passed out where I was. Who the hell just said that? Surely not the man whatever it was (I could not even bring myself to accept his dead state). It sounded like a voice from the radio or like a static walkie-talkie sound.

"Me hear you loud and clear man, you take me bwaay, me come fe ya. Ya family, ya people, me gat all ya names. Me hear it all...static sound...Me the Lord master Akalango. Me no send me acolytes out on their own."

"Since ya heard it all, then hear this, me family nah do yah nuttin. You send ya rude bwaay acolyte into me home to ruin and scar all dah lives of innocent people. If ya strong as ya claim you be, ya fi don take Delis ah long time. Me gaan take ya fi bury alongside Sokoni...me give you one last chance of life now." Elder Dumayi spoke so authoritatively and fearlessly.

If it was not all such a horrible situation, I would have been proud.

Then with what seemed like a roar elder Dumayi said, "I am the soul of Akalamavon river, me the life source, the length and breadth of it. Anything comes there drowns..."

"The soul of Akalamavon river?" the so-called Lord master asked through the static sound. I picked up a hint of fear in his voice.

"Why ya na say that first, me for take away me acolyte...we still need sort this out with Lord Zukan the highest Lord," he added quickly.

"You do that...ask Lord Zee about me. You cam clear up dis mess you cause me to make. For ya sake I been exposed to me family. For that you pay dearly." Elder Dumayi said harshly.

"El-dee, El-dee...hailings man...El-dee!" Lord master said and with that there was a loud bang in the corridor.

Then I lost consciousness.

Chapter 4

The Harsh Reality

I must have fainted. I still don't know what really happened. I woke up this morning and everything seemed normal - we-all-slept-in-our-beds kind of normal. I saw mum and said hello to her as I walked into the kitchen for breakfast. She was making scrambled eggs.

"Hi mum," I said.

"Hey babe, how's that little monkey?" She asked. "You slept right through the fireworks display that we had for Uncle Sparkie. The baby must have worn you out."

"Fireworks!!" I said surprised.

"Yes fireworks," mum said looking puzzled. Don't tell me you have also forgotten we were having it. You signed the delivery yesterday morning.

It was all news to me. I looked in the direction of the bin and saw the empty cartons from the said fireworks. I made black coffee instead of my usual tea as I sat down to make sense of everything. This morning certainly needed something stronger.

"Should you be drinking that?" mum asked as I took a sip from the cup.

"How about sister and everyone?" I asked ignoring her question.

"They all left after the display yesterday. Your husband called earlier, his flight arrives later today. I hope you have not forgotten that too?" she asked.

Well, as you may have guessed, I had!

Did I bang my head? All that last night... that was surely not a dream?

I rang my sister after my bath, and she also talked about how cool the fireworks display was.

"Are you okay sis?" she asked me.

"Sure...why?" I asked.

"Well, you were out like a light too early last night. I did come to get you, but you did not even flinch. Sorry but I can't help but notice that you sound so surprised about the fireworks. You made a big fuss about signing for that delivery," she concluded.

"I am just tired," I replied.

"Okay take care of you baby girl," sis Jumi said.

"I will ... bye," and with that I hung up.

The doorbell rang and I was just breastfeeding my baby by the balcony. My mum got the door. I could hear her greet my uncle Elder Dumayi.

"Good morning sir," I screamed out from where I was as he approached me. I sat transfixed and panic stricken as he walked towards me. It was such bad timing for me, as I could not move with my baby sucking away hungrily.

"Good morning blessed child," he said as he always did.

"How is the baby? And hey... why did you sleep like a log of wood last night? Are you okay Perry?" he asked lowering himself towards me where I sat on the floor with the baby at my bosom. He cupped my chin in his palm, lifting my face up and looking straight into my eyes. It felt like he was looking for clues in my eyes...or so I thought. I could not meet his gaze. I curled away, lifting my baby as I did.

"Yes sir, I was ...j-just tired," I stammered trying to hide my uneasiness. I could not stop thinking about him last night...or was it all a dream? I was so confused. My head ached.

"I hope that guy has not knocked you up again, has he? I will have words with him. You still nursing this little man!" he said regarding me.

We both laughed.

"No, my darling uncle, have no fear," I said allowing myself to relax. He was still my uncle. Our good old Elder Dumayi. He was no killer or Lord or anything. It all felt so scary. My uncle went in looking for his baby brother, as he liked to call my dad. It was funny how much that statement offended my dad.

Later in the evening my husband arrived. Mom did not even let the guy rest. She filled him in on the party, fireworks, and fun. I still secretly listened carefully to hear if any sinister hints were going to be dropped.

But nothing...

It was all in my head then, I concluded.

When we finally had a moment, I told Tendayi my husband and soul mate all about what happened.

"Hmm, the dreamer," he teased. "You do look tired," he added.

"I am dear, but it was so real, so frightfully real, I am still a bit unsettled," I told him.

He cradled me in his arms reassuringly.

"Don't worry love it will pass. Dreams always fade with time. We just perhaps have to warn Delis to be more careful. Just in case what you saw in your dream was a sign of danger," he said.

That made sense.

"Hmmm, it could all have been a sign." I echoed his words silently to myself. Tendayi asked me to get ready so that we could leave. He had missed me so much. Moreover, we needed our own space to show each other how much we missed each other.

"What a relief," I thought. I strolled happily to the kitchen to get my boy's milk. I heard voices as I walked down the corridor leading to the kitchen.

"Look here Delis, I only came to warn you," my uncle's voice threatened. I froze at once recognising that scary tone in his voice.

"Yes sir, thank you sir" Delis stammered.

"You won't be thanking me next time," my uncle Elder Dumayi said coldly.

"Can you see what you made me do? I had to go back in time to alter the sequence. Who knows, I may have disrupted the balance in time. These things have consequences. We can only wait and see. The next time you decide to make trouble, do not... I repeat do not drag it to our doorstep you fool!" he snapped.

"I won't sir El-dee, I won't sir," Delis sounded dreadfully frightened. I had the inclination to walking and asking what the palaver was, but my common sense held me back.

"There should never be a next time," elder Dumayi said. "What did I say?" He asked Delis.

"You said that there should never be a next time," Delis replied.

"Repeat it!" My uncle ordered.

"You said that there should never be a next time sir!" Delis repeated.

"Good!" My uncle said.

"If there ever is, it will be you in that trunk not that Sokoni. Do I make myself clear?" Elder Dumayi threatened.

"Yes sir," Delis responded.

I quickly made a U-turn back to the living room where my husband was and tried staying composed.

"Did you not get the bottle anymore?" Tendayi asked me.

"What bottle? Oh! I completely forgot as I got distracted by one of those cold callers on the telephone," I lied.

"Okay, hurry up then so we can leave," he said.

I just slumped into the chair feigning exhaustion.

"I feel really tired babe," I said trying to delay going back into that kitchen.

I watched Tendayi play with baby and tried to let that view of them playing settle me. Soon enough Delis walked into the living room with a bottle of coke. He looked frightened. He dropped his bottle on the side table next to him, slumped into the soft sofa and appeared to have fallen asleep. I knew he was not asleep. I knew he was so scared to death. I also knew I wanted to stay out of it. I needed to leave and pretend I did not hear all I had just heard.

The End.

A short story by Lauretta Ofulue rendered with gentleness. This is different from her usual storytelling but a welcome addition that demonstrates her versatility in writing - **Michael Noble**.

Lauretta helps the reader experience the reality of how simple events can have alternative explanations - **Remiah Chuk**

In this book a young lady enjoys a lovely day with her family before a knock on the door challenges her understanding about her family as she knows it. It gives her insights into what may be a secret, but she can't be sure

Lauretta Ofulue is a Christian. She is often described as feisty, determined and too kind by close friends and other family members. Lauretta is also a mother. She also feels lucky to share her life everyday with her childhood sweetheart and husband. She describes their relationship as her most successful career. Lauretta spends most of her time writing, sewing, walking, singing, dancing and colouring. She lives with her family in Buckinghamshire, England.

She is also a multiple award-winning nurse, Public speaker, and a Catechism teacher.

www.ingramcontent.com/pod-product-compliance
Lightning Source LLC
LaVergne TN
LVHW080629160826
845677LV00007B/1487

* 9 7 9 8 3 7 2 2 0 1 2 2 4 *